In memory of my grandfather, Edwin Bobiney
And for my grandmother, Adelaide—a lady I adore
—K.D.

To my grandparents, for making the journey to liberty
—R.E.

Text copyright © 2004 by Kelly DiPucchio

Illustrations copyright © 2004 by Richard Egielski

First Edition

This book is set in 18-point Academy Engraved.

1 3 5 7 9 10 8 6 4 2

ISBN 0-7868-1876-X

Printed in Singapore

Reinforced binding

Library of Congress Cataloging-in-Publication Data on file.

Visit www.hyperionbooksforchildren.com

Liberty's Journey

Kelly DiPucchio

ILLUSTRATIONS BY
Richard Egielski

HYPERION BOOKS FOR CHILDREN
NEW YORK

Upon a salt-licked island shore
stands a lady folks adore.
A mighty beacon by the sea,
she greets the tired, the poor, the free.

But one day, Lady Liberty
wished that she could roam and see
the people who had come and gone;
the land they built their dreams upon.

So, early on that foggy morn,
before the ferry's echoed horn,
she stepped down from her sacred place
and disappeared without a trace.

Careful of the island trees,
she pulled her gown up to her knees,
then waded 'cross the steel-blue bay—
her bold adventure underway.

She tiptoed down dark, sleepy streets,
past bakers selling bread and sweets.
Through neighborhoods and alleyways,
she zigzagged through the city maze.

Walking west against the sky,
the Lady cautiously stepped by
a rusty map of railroad track,
the sunrise blooming at her back.

In search of amber waves of grain,
she trekked beside a chugging train
through patchwork fields of green and brown—
white cherry blossoms in her crown.

She came upon a county fair.
People paused to point and stare.
The Ferris wheel slowed to a stop.
A little girl called from the top,

"Hello, Miss Lady Liberty!
My nana waved to you from the sea.
She came here on a crowded boat
with just her doll and tattered coat."

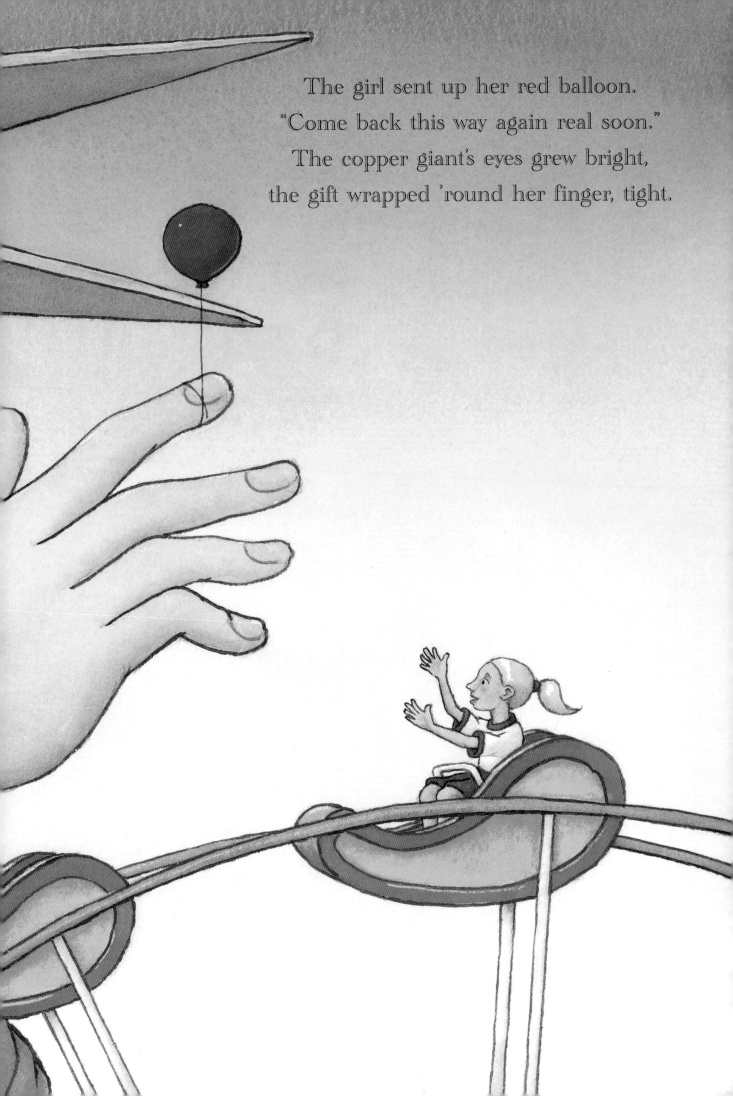

The girl sent up her red balloon.
"Come back this way again real soon."
The copper giant's eyes grew bright,
the gift wrapped 'round her finger, tight.

Back at home, distraught since dawn
to find their lovely lady gone,
New Yorkers searched both far and wide.
"Where *could* a woman that tall hide?"

Still the Lady traveled on,
not tired, sad, or woebegone;
her joy renewed by distant places
filled with children's hopeful faces.

Crowds grew bigger day by day,
escorting her along the way.
Ranchers cheered when she arrived
behind a dusty cattle drive.

Across the nighttime desert sand,
the Lady's torch glowed in her hand.
While canyon creatures sang a tune,
she nestled 'neath a marble moon.

News of Liberty's whereabouts
filled New York with happy shouts.
They put in place a clever plan,
calling forth her every fan.

Out west, their wayward Liberty
stood beside a redwood tree;
her destination now in sight,
warm waters spilling waves of white.

People on the golden bridge
watched her lumber down a ridge.
At long last, Lady Liberty
had journeyed sea to shining sea.

She smelled the fragrant ocean air;
Pacific breezes tossed her hair.
Ships and sailboats welcomed her,
but in her heart—a lonely stir.

She missed Manhattan's sounds and sights.
She missed the city's brilliant lights.
She missed the harbor ferry's horn.
She missed her home, where hope was born.

"Excuse me," said a boy in blue.
"This mail arrived, addressed to you."
Inside his heavy canvas sack
were cards and letters:
"Please come back!"

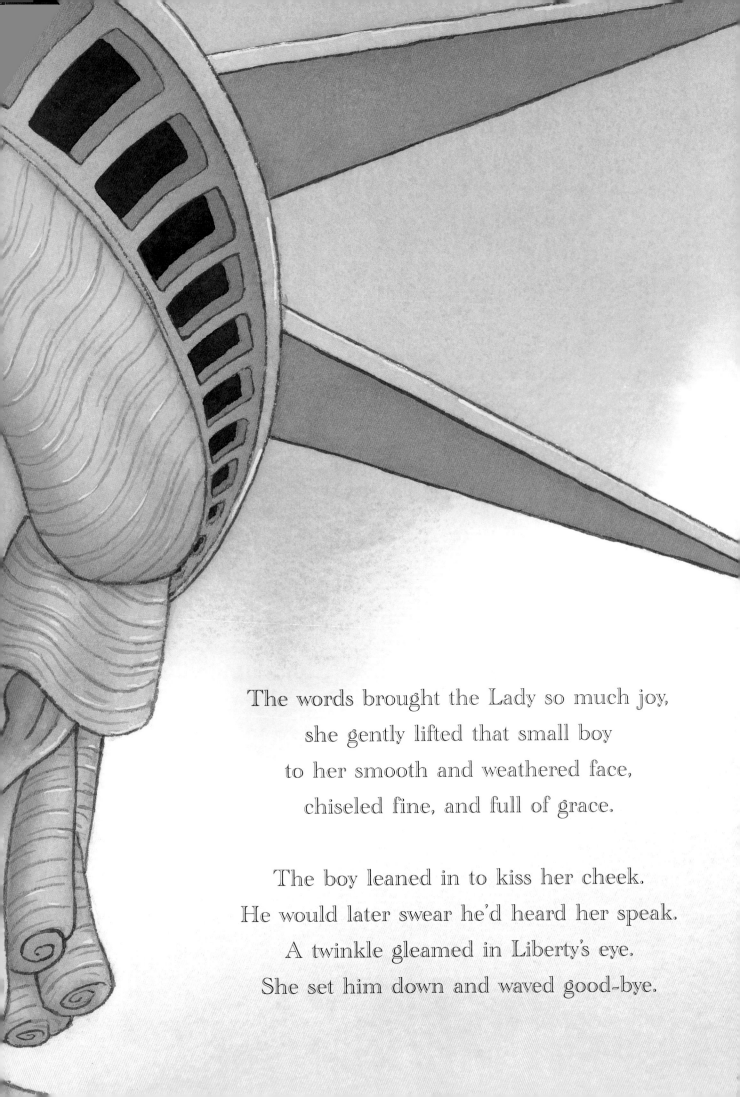

The words brought the Lady so much joy,
she gently lifted that small boy
to her smooth and weathered face,
chiseled fine, and full of grace.

The boy leaned in to kiss her cheek.
He would later swear he'd heard her speak.
A twinkle gleamed in Liberty's eye.
She set him down and waved good-bye.

She traveled 'cross the fruited plain,
through canyons, Black Hills, northern rain.
New Yorkers lined the cityscape
with floats and bands and ticker tape.

Firefighters, kind and brave,
stopped their trucks to cheer and wave.
The Lady greeted everyone;
her faith restored, her journey done.

Back upon her salt-licked shore
stands the Lady, proud once more.
Our faithful beacon by the sea
is home where she was meant to be.

★ Author's Note ★

THE STATUE OF LIBERTY is one of the most recognizable symbols of freedom and democracy in the United States and around the world. Standing at the entrance to New York Harbor, this colossal iron-framed, copper-clad statue was a gift of friendship from the people of France. In 1865, French historian Édouard de Laboulaye came up with a plan to present a gift to commemorate America's one hundredth anniversary of independence. Originally known as *Liberty Enlightening the World,* the statue was designed and built in Paris by French sculptor Frédéric-Auguste Bartholdi; her structural frame was designed by Alexandre-Gustave Eiffel, architect of the Eiffel Tower.

While the statue was being constructed overseas, the United States began work on the enormous pedestal on Bedloe's Island. In 1883, Emma Lazarus wrote her famous poem, *The New Colossus,* as part of a fund-raising effort to pay for the 89-foot pedestal. Back in France, the completed statue was presented to the American people in a ceremony on July 4, 1884. In 1885, the gigantic statue was dismantled and shipped in 214 crates to the United States. The Statue of Liberty was officially dedicated on October 28, 1886. In 1903, *The New Colossus* was inscribed on the statue's pedestal. It wasn't until October 15, 1924, that the Statue of Liberty was designated as a National Monument. In 1956, Bedloe's Island was officially renamed Liberty Island. Lady Liberty was extensively restored for her one hundredth birthday and rededicated in an elaborate ceremony on October 28, 1986.

A closer look at the Statue of Liberty reveals several symbols important to the United States. The broken chain at her feet represents America's freedom from oppression. The seven rays on her crown are said to represent the seven seas and the seven continents. In her left hand, Lady Liberty holds the Declaration of Independence. The 23-foot tablet is inscribed *July 4, 1776* in Roman numerals. In her right hand, Lady Liberty holds a torch of freedom that welcomes people from all lands.

If the Statue of Liberty did take a stroll through your town, she'd be hard to miss! She stands a remarkable 151 feet tall. Her nose is a whopping 4 feet 6 inches long and her mouth stretches 3 feet wide. Experts have calculated that Lady Liberty's huge 25-foot feet would require sandals in an astounding size 879! There's no doubt that Miss Liberty would leave some impressive footprints if she walked across America.

THE NEW COLOSSUS

Not like the brazen giant of Greek fame,
With conquering limbs astride from land to land;
Here at our sea-washed, sunset gates shall stand
A mighty woman with a torch, whose flame
Is the imprisoned lightning, and her name
Mother of Exiles. From her beacon-hand
Glows world-wide welcome; her mild eyes command
The air-bridged harbor that twin cities frame,
"Keep, ancient lands, your storied pomp!" cries she
With silent lips. "Give me your tired, your poor,
Your huddled masses yearning to breathe free,
The wretched refuse of your teeming shore,
Send these, the homeless, tempest-tost to me,
I lift my lamp beside the golden door!"